MY ANIMAL ANTICS BOOK

CONTENTS :

Fifi's Adventure
Mischievous Misty
The Cheeky Jumbos
Benny and Butch
Goldilocks and the three Bears

"Come and play with us Fifi," says one of his brothers next morning.

"Let's find some juicy worms," says another.

Fifi says nothing, because he is too busy thinking. And he thinks of only one thing.

"How I would love to fly like the Eagle up above the mountain-tops and talk to the sun!"

Suddenly Michael and his sister Sally come running out of the house and... Whirr! All the sparrows scatter quickly. But they don't fly far away, because they are very curious about something Michael is holding.

In fact he has a beautiful kite that his father has given him for his birthday; a kite that looks to the little sparrows just like one of those great birds that hover high in the clouds.

Sally is carrying a bobbin of string.

Fifi is very puzzled by this strange new bird. Might

it be the Eagle that Mr. Know-All talked about?

"Where shall we go?" calls out Sally.

"In the open field where there aren't any trees to tangle the string," shouts Michael.

And on they run. Fifi never lets them out of his sight. Sometimes he flies in front of them, sometimes behind, but always his eyes are fixed on that strange bird in Michael's hand.

And here we are at last in the open fields. Today

there is a fresh wind that sends the clouds chasing each other across the blue sky and bends the stalks of corn and barley nearly flat against the ground.

"Which way is the wind coming from?" asks Michael. "Ah good, from the west. Come here Sally: you hold the kite here like this. I shall run into the wind. When I say 'Now', let go. But first I must make sure the string is well tied on."

Fifi looks on in wonder.

Fifi is becoming more and more puzzled. The big

bird doesn't seem to be able to move or hear or speak. He lets himself be carried about by the children and allows them to tie bits of string to his wings without saying a word! Perhaps it is not an Eagle after all.... perhaps it can't fly. ... perhaps it's a dead Eagle....

Michael is already in the middle of the field.

Suddenly there is a great gust of wind that almost pulls the kite from Sally's hands.

"Now!" shouts Michael.

Sally lets go of the kite and in a moment the wind has caught it and tugged it into the air. Fifi is delighted to see that the great bird can really fly. He loops the loop and claps his wings with joy. Slowly the great bird climbs up and up.

"I wonder how high he will fly," thinks Fifi. "Oh! if only I could be there with him!"

But how can he? Fifi has only very short wings and he can't possibly climb when such a strong wind

is blowing. Suddenly he has an idea: he shoots upwards and perches on the back of the great bird.

"What a funny back! What ever are these wooden struts for? Still, they're very handy for clinging on to."

Still the kite climbs. Soon it's as high as the top of the tallest poplar tree, where a family of crows are holding a party for one of their cousins who has just got married.

"What's this, what's this?" says the father crow.

"What do you think you're doing here, young sparrow? You weren't invited to our party."

Fifi puts his beak in the air and says proudly: "Please don't disturb yourselves. I was just passing by!"

Higher and higher soars the kite. Fifi stops for a chat with a very startled skylark who thought nobody could fly as high as he could. Then the sparrow and the great bird are quite alone in the sky, high above the trees and fields.

Fifi is fairly bursting with happiness: he is flying

on the back of the Eagle, the King of Birds, Master of the Skies!

But before long Fifi begins to feel a little uneasy. Really, the sky is so quiet and empty... and rather frightening.

Yes; now he is afraid, and cold too. He puffs up his feathers to keep warm. When will they start going down again? If only he had broad wings to glide with, or if he could dive like a skylark!

Fifi becomes more and more frightened. How he longs to be back on the ground again with his brothers

and sisters, back in his snug little nest.

And this great bird that can't hear anything and never speaks, will it never fly down to the ground again? The more he thinks about it, the more certain Fifi is that the whole thing has been a trap for him. Eagle indeed! Fifi closes his eyes, feeling very sorry for himself. He's hungry, cold, tired, and very miserable. He'll probably die up there all alone in the empty sky.

It is evening now and the sun is beginning to sink out of sight. Poor Fifi is still there, drifting among the clouds!

"I'm getting tired now," says Sally.

"Me too," says Michael. "Holding the kite in this wind is making my arms ache."

"Shall we go home then?"

"Yes, that's enough for one day. Besides, it's getting dark. I'm going to try to wind the kite in."

Gently Michael pulls at the string and starts to wind it back on to the bobbin. Slowly, very slowly, the kite comes down. Fifi, who was dozing miserably, is jerked awake by its movement and opens his eyes. Strange, he doesn't feel half so bad now! The air is getting warmer.

And what's that he sees underneath him? It's the ground, and it's getting nearer and nearer! He has never been more pleased to see the trees and fields.

Fifi does not care where the big bird will land and what the children will do with it. He has flown back to his brothers long before it touches the ground.

"Wherever have you been Fifi?"

"We called out and looked for you everywhere."

"Where were you hiding?"

"I...I lost my way," says Fifi blushing slightly, "and it has taken me such a long time to find my way back home. But never mind that: let's go and play and find some nice juicy worms!"

That evening Fifi is bursting to tell Mr. Know-All about the day's adventure. The old owl listens with his eyes closed, and from time to time he nods his head.

"Well Fifi," he says with a smile when the sparrow has finished, "you understand now that birds like you and me must keep to our own homes. We mustn't all hope to be Eagles. You have learned your lesson, and now you must go to bed. It is time I went hunting."

MISCHIEVOUS MISTY
by M. Englebert and Chader

Coming back from a walk one day, Anne and her father find a little kitten miaowing on the doorstep of their house.

"Perhaps he is hungry," says Father.

"Would you like a saucer of milk, little kitten?"

The little kitten certainly thinks this is a good idea, for he purrs and rubs himself against Father's leg.

"Oh Daddy, please may I keep him?" asks Anne, picking the kitten up in her arms. "We shall call him Misty."

Mother opens her eyes wide in surprise when she sees the kitten nestled in Anne's arms.

"We found him on the doorstep and now he's ours," says Anne firmly, before Mother has time to speak!

They put Misty on the carpet and he sits there not quite knowing what to do next. He has beautiful golden eyes, a grey and black coat, and fine pointed ears that twitch when Anne speaks to him.

Mother fetches a saucer of creamy milk for him. Misty is so thirsty that he splashes the milk all over his chin as he is lapping it up!

The sitting-room is very much what he likes, because in it there's a cosy red chair with a blue cushion. Red and blue are his favourite colours, and the chair looks so comfortable, so he jumps up and settles down for a nap.

"Really!" says Father; "Cats ought to sleep in their baskets."

But Misty just opens his pretty red mouth to yawn, closes his eyes, and goes off to sleep.

Misty wakes up next morning feeling very happy.

Anne is delighted to see him. She cuddles him and sits him down next to her black doll, Elizabeth.

"Now we shall play at being in school," says Anne talking to all the toys: "I will be the teacher."

But what a naughty pupil Misty is! He turns his back to the blackboard, rolls on his back, and scampers all round the room after a piece of chalk. He won't be still for a moment.

Anne can't help laughing at him, although she tries

to look stern. The other dolls are pleased too, because they don't much like this sort of game. Teddy Bear hates learning to read, and it's fun to have such a mischievous kitten spoiling all the lessons. Misty jumps on to the cot and sniffs at the white doll.

"Since you have been such a mischievous Misty," says Anne wagging a finger at him, "you must be punished."

And she locks him in the bathroom. Of course, Misty doesn't mind a bit. He jumps on to the wash-basin and catches the drops of water as they fall.

"But I thought kittens didn't like water," says Anne with surprise when she opens the door again.

"Miaow, I do!" says Misty.

Now it's time for Anne's bath. Water in a bath is something new to Misty. I wonder how deep it is... He stretches out a paw carefully... Splash!

"You silly, silly wet kitten," laughs Anne giving him a hug.

Poor Misty, he looks so wet and unhappy! He shakes himself and sneezes, and Mother wipes him with her apron.

Next morning Father is up bright and early to paint the garden wall.

"Now I must see this," says Misty.

Up the ladder he goes, jumping from rung to rung, until suddenly his back paws slip and he is hanging by his tummy!

"What a mischievous rascal!" says Father helping him down safely again.

And now he goes to explore the rest of the garden.

"Tweet, tweet," whistles the blackbird.

Misty is quite sure that the blackbird is poking fun at him. He must be taught a lesson. The kitten flattens himself against the grass and crouches, ready to spring. All the time he glares (as fiercely as a kitten can) at the bird perched in the old cherry tree.

"Tweet, tweet, you'll never catch me, Misty!"

Never mind the cheeky young blackbird : there are more places to be explored, thinks Misty. So he jumps on to the garden wall, and below him sees Dick, the neighbour's dog, digging a hole in the ground. Dick lifts his head and growls at him because the kitten has stopped the important job he is doing.

"Bow, wow, wow!" barks the dog, standing with his two front paws against the wall.

Misty puffs up the fur on his back and hisses loudly.

"You are not a very polite kitten, you know," says Dick in between barks : "why are you hissing at me like that?"

"I hiss at everyone I don't know," says Misty.

"Well, you know me now. My name is Dick. Shall we be friends?"

Misty is very pleased indeed to be friends with Dick, and climbs down on to the lilac bush to chat with him.

In the evening, when Dick is snoring in his kennel and the moon is shining, Misty goes for a walk along the garden paths.

Even then he isn't tired of games. He tumbles about on the grass and plays hide-and-seek with his shadow. He sits on the flower-beds chatting with other cats, and sniffs each flower in turn to see which smells nicest.

Next morning, at breakfast, Misty slips into a chair beside Anne and miaows gently.

"Do you want some chocolate, dear? There, that's for you."

And she gives him a delicious piece of chocolate.

Misty, standing up on his back legs, takes the chocolate. He eats it greedily, smacks his lips, and miaows for more!

When Anne gets up from her chair, Misty clings tightly to her blouse, jumps on to her shoulder and ruffles her hair. He has decided to be mischievous today! Anne would love to play with him, but she must go off to school. So Misty goes with Mother to the door, and together they wave to Anne until she is out of sight.

"Bye, bye, Misty. Promise me you'll be good. And don't break anything!"

Misty curls up into a little ball and goes to sleep. He dreams he is the Prince of Kittens, with a gold crown and a flowing red cape. He is marching grandly in front of the mice, who are all bowing before him. Then he wakes up. Oh dear, it was only a dream!

"All the same," says the kitten as he admires himself in the mirror and combs out his whiskers, "I *am* as handsome as a prince."

The window is open and a gentle breeze is playing with the curtains. You know kittens love anything that moves: well, Misty is watching those curtains all the time. All at once he springs up and clings to a curtain with his claws.

"Come down at once you naughty kitten!"

Mother has seen him swinging to and fro on her best curtains and she is very cross. She opens the door.

"Go on, into the garden with you. And stay there."

Misty scampers out of doors with his tail between his legs. He can hear Dick barking next door.

Dick has a brand new collar with his name on it.

"I shan't ever get lost with this collar round my neck," he explains. "But haven't you got one too, Misty?"

"Don't be silly," says Misty. "A cat doesn't have to be taken for walks. He is free. He does what he likes. And he isn't tied up with a lead and a collar."

With this, Misty stretches out comfortably on the wall in the warm sunlight, yawns, and goes off to sleep.

THE CHEEKY JUMBOS
by M. Vérité and R. Simon

"Hold on to my tail, Huff," ordered Mother Jumbo.

"Puff and I want to stay here and play!" cried Huff.

"You do as you're told," replied Mother Jumbo.

Every time their parents wanted to move on to find some fresh grass the two scamps could never be found.

"All right, children, you can go and play now," said

Father Jumbo, who had found some lovely fresh grass to eat.

"Remember, don't go too far away," warned Mother Jumbo. "King Lion and Lord Leopard live near here."

Of course, Huff and Puff did just what they were told not to.

Forgetting their parents' warning they dashed off. Huff was first.

·"Come on, slow coach," joked Huff. "Let's see what we can find."

As he said this Puff dashed past him into some bushes.

He did not go far.

Lazing in the sun was Lord Leopard.

"And where do you think you are going?" growled Lord Leopard.

"We...we...we are only playing," cried Puff.

"Well, get back to your Mother and Father before I get very angry," said Lord Leopard.

Huff and Puff did not need to be told twice!

At midday they went down to the river.

"Now you two," ordered Father Jumbo, "don't tease Baby Hippo."

Huff and Puff had not spotted Old Razor-tooth, the Crocodile. But he had spotted them.

Old Razor-tooth was looking for his dinner.

He was always hungry.

"I can squirt higher than you," shouted Puff.

" We'll soon see," replied Huff.

By this time Old Razor-tooth had silently floated to within a few feet of Puff.

"They'd better not," grumbled Father Hippo, remembering the last time the two scamps had squirted Baby Hippo.

Huff and Puff also remembered it, for Father Hippo had chased them along the river bank.

Huff and Puff played by themselves.

"Out of the way!" snorted the leader of the Buffalo Family.

Huff and Puff stopped playing and moved quickly towards the bank.

They did not want to annoy the Buffaloes. They knew that they had very bad tempers and loved to have a fight.

The Buffalo Family were not interested in Huff
and Puff.

They were on their way to find some fresh food.

Snap!!!

Old Razor-tooth struck.

"Help! Help! Help!" yelled Puff.

Father and Mother Jumbo dashed into the river.

"Run to the bank," cried Mother Jumbo.

Puff was so frightened that he ran the wrong way.
"Mummy, Mummy!" cried Puff.
"This way! This way!" bellowed Father Jumbo.
Puff stopped and ran crying to his Mother.
Father Jumbo looked around for Old Razor-tooth,
but he had silently swum away with the end of
Puff's tail between his teeth.

"Oh, poor Puff, poor Puff," cried Huff with big tears in his eyes.

"Don't make too much fuss," said Mother Jumbo. "If you hadn't wandered off this would not have happened."

"Come on everyone," ordered Father Jumbo.

"Where are we going?" asked Puff, already forgetting about his tail.

"Into the jungle to find some nice fresh fruit," replied Father Jumbo.

Puff had now forgotten all about his tail.

"Look, there's Tommy Zebra," shouted Puff.

"Let's chase him," called Huff.

"Follow us, you two," ordered Father Jumbo. "We have a long way to walk."

Huff and Puff fell in behind their parents and

did not stop until they reached the jungle.

"Children, now watch where you are going,"
said Father Jumbo.

"It's a bit creepy in here," whispered Huff.

"Don't be silly," replied Mother Jumbo.

"Let's pick some flowers, Huff," said Puff.

"You leave the flowers alone. You may pick

up a snake by mistake and find his bite much worse than Old Razor-tooth's," warned Father Jumbo.

Huff and Puff kept close to their parents until they came to a pool.

"Let's have a bathe," said Huff.

Puff was not at all certain.

"Don't worry, Puff," said Father Jumbo. "Old Razor-tooth is not in this pool."

"Come on in," called Huff.

Carefully Puff stepped into the water.

In no time at all he was romping and squirting water over Huff.

"Come on, children, we can't spend all day here," called Father Jumbo.

But they could not do as they were told. They chased each other until Huff fell into a hole.

Puff curled his trunk round Huff's and pulled and pulled.

Puff did his best but he had to wait for his Father to help him.

At last the Jumbo Family came to a part of the jungle where the trees were loaded down with lovely red fruit.

"Don't eat too many," warned Mother Jumbo.

"Remember, children, there is always another day," added Father Jumbo.

"Shoo away, shoo away!" shouted Puff at the birds pecking at the fruit.

"Leave them alone," ordered Mother Jumbo. "There is plenty for everyone."

"They're trying to peck my trunk," cried Puff.

"Poor Puff," teased Huff. "He lost the tip of his tail and now he's afraid of losing the tip of his trunk."

"Enough squabbling, you two," ordered Father Jumbo. "We must get back before dark."

Off dashed Huff and Puff.

"I'll race you back," called Puff.

"And I'll beat you," replied Huff.

"Be careful—and don't fall in that hole again," called Father Jumbo.

Of course, they did not hear one word.

All they cared about was getting back to the long grass to play with their friends.

"I can reach higher than you," said Huff.

"No you can't," shouted Puff.

The two scamps were up to their pranks again.

BENNY AND BUTCH

by J. Cappe and M. Marlier

"Oh, my goodness!" said Mrs Rabbit. "Oh, my goodness, I really don't know what to do. You're three months old now, and I still can't tell you apart!"

"I'm Butch," said Benny.

"I'm Benny," said Butch.

"Then who left this carrot on the floor?" said Mrs Rabbit, pointing at it.

"Benny did," said Butch, who had just said that his name was Benny.

"Right," said Mrs Rabbit, "I'm going to the village to buy a blue ribbon and a red ribbon; then I'll know who's who. You two can just stay here!"

So off went Mrs Rabbit to the village, and two minutes
later, off went Butch and Benny in the other direction.

"Where shall we go?" said Benny.

"Well, we've never got right to the House," answered
Butch. "Let's go there."

"I don't know if we should," said Benny, who was a bit

more careful than his brother. But in the end they went in the direction of the House, which was quite an ordinary farmhouse; of course, for the two little rabbits, it was something very special.

On the way, they passed Basil and little black-faced Bertha, the two lambs.

"We're going to the House," cried the two little rabbits. "Would you like to come?"

"Not likely," they replied. "We like it here, where there's plenty of grass to eat." And they both jumped up and down as lambs do.

"Come on," said Butch to Benny. "We'll go on our own."

It wasn't long before they came to the garden of the House, and there, outside, was a great big bucket of whitewash.

"Oh, look!" said Butch. "A bucket of milk."

So they both poked their noses in it!

"Ugh!" said Butch.

"Ugh!" said Benny.

They looked at each other, and rubbed their noses.

"It won't come off," they said together.

Just then, along came Billy on his scooter. He got to the bottom of the path when he saw the two little rabbits with whitewash all over their noses.

"Oh, look at that!" he said, and burst out laughing.

But he would have done better to look where he was going. Before he knew it, he went straight into the cabbage patch!

It was Benny's and Butch's turn to laugh.

"What a pity, though," said Butch. "He's spoiled half the juicy cabbages."

"What shall we do now?" asked Benny.

"Have a look at the lawn over there by the flower-bed," said Butch quietly. "What can you see?"

"Ooh!" squeaked Benny. "A monster-carrot!"
The two little rabbits went off like rockets!
"I'll beat you there," said Butch, going like the wind.
"Oh, no you won't," said Benny.

They both arrived together, and saw that another
rabbit was holding the carrot.

"Is that yours?" asked Butch.

The other rabbit didn't reply.

"Can we have a bite?" asked Benny.

Still no reply.

"It's not real," said Butch.

"Let's eat the carrot then," said Benny.

Butch immediately took a bite.

Bang!

It wasn't a real carrot either!

Butch and Benny both fell over backwards in surprise.

"I don't think this is a very good place," said Butch.

"You never know what's going to happen next!"

So they both turned, and dashed off back down the road, looking around all the time to make sure that no other funny things were following them!

They didn't stop running until they reached home.

Mrs Rabbit was waiting for them.

"What on earth have you got on your faces?" she said.

The two little rabbits knew they had been rather naughty.

"Well, we saw a bucket of milk," said Butch.

"And we were rather thirsty," went on Benny.

"So we had a drink, but it wasn't milk," finished off Butch.

"You silly little rabbits," said Mrs Rabbit. "You should never drink things when you're not sure what they are. Right, into the tub with you."

And into the tub they went. Mrs Rabbit scrubbed and scrubbed, but . . .

"Oh dear, I suppose we'll just have to wait until your whiskers grow, and then we can cut it off," she said.

When they were dry, she put the new ribbons on them — a red one for Butch, and a blue one for Benny.

The two little rabbits got quite used to their white noses, and were even sorry when the day came for their whiskers to be trimmed!

GOLDILOCKS AND THE THREE BEARS

by L. Berger and S. Baudoin

What an inquisitive child Goldilocks was! She fiddled with everything, climbed on chairs, looked in drawers.

Her mother had told her not to a hundred times, but it was no use. She wanted to see everything, to know everything. . . .

She even wanted to walk alone in the woods before she was really old enough. And one day when her mother was baking a cake, she slipped out of the house and took the path through the trees, amongst the birds and the flowers. Further and further she went into the forest.

"Now I'd better go home," thought Goldilocks. But suddenly she saw a little wooden house with its roof covered with straw.

"I wonder who lives there?" Goldilocks asked herself.

And she was so curious that, instead of going home, she walked up to the little house to get a better look. The door to the garden was ajar, so she pushed it open, and went in.

The garden was full of flowers and beehives. Goldilocks went into the house, and saw a long table with three bowls on it: one large, one medium, one small. By the table were three stools: one large, one medium, one small.

"This stool is too high for me," said Goldilocks, as she tried to sit on the large one.

She dropped down onto the small one. "Oh! This one is too low!" she cried.

Then she sat on the middle one. "Ah! This one is just right."

"Now let's see what's in the bowls," she said. "Ah, it's porridge — I must taste a bit. No one will notice a little missing from the large bowl . . . oh, not enough sugar! Let's try the small bowl . . . oh, that's far too sweet! And the middle one? Ah, just how I like it," she thought, and ate it all down.

When she had finished, she ran upstairs. In the bedroom, there were three beds: one large, one medium and one small. Goldilocks climbed onto the large one. "Ooh, this one's too hard," she said, and lay down on the small bed.

"Oh, no," she said, "this one's far too soft . . . let's try the middle one. Aah, how comfy it is!" And she slid underneath the eiderdown.

"I wonder who lives in this house?" she mused again. Then all of a sudden she didn't think any more. She was so tired, she simply fell asleep.

Well, who would have thought it? Three bears lived in the house with red shutters: Brian the large bear, Betty the medium bear and Bobo the small bear.

They had gone for a stroll in the forest to let their dinner cool down, but now they were coming back.

They each took their own stool. Brian sat down on the large one; Betty had to sit up on her knees on her medium one; and Bobo stood up on his small stool. It was a funny sight!

But alas, when Betty saw that her bowl was empty, she began to cry. "Someone has eaten all my porridge!" she said, as she wiped her eyes on her napkin.

Brian and Bobo kindly shared their porridge with Betty, but she was still upset.

"Who has eaten my dinner?" she kept saying, as she dried away her tears.

After dinner they looked inside the clock, behind the cooker and even under the kitchen sink, but found nobody.

Bobo went to see the bees. "I bet you ate my sister's porridge," he said.

Betty was tired — she had worked all morning in the garden.

"I'm going to have a nap," she told Brian. Then she put her slippers on and went upstairs. Brian began to wash up the three bowls and three spoons.

Entering the bedroom, Betty saw that there was someone in her bed. She tiptoed up close, and shook poor Goldilocks wide awake.

"Come and see what I've found!" she called to the other bears. "A little girl has come to say hello!" Brian and Bobo ran upstairs, eager to meet their visitor.

But Goldilocks jumped up, and without even pausing to put on her shoes she fled down the stairs. She ran home as fast as she could, and she was never as curious ever again. When she was older, she went for long walks in the forest, but the three bears were no longer there. Now they live in town, in the zoo where *you* can meet them and say hello!

80

Printed in Belgium by CASTERMAN S.A.